Longlisted for the

CILIP Kate Greenaway Medal 2013

"An ingenious, thought-provoking picture book

that allows children to be both good and bad."

– The Sunday Times

A TEMPLAR BOOK

First published in the UK in 2012 by Templar Publishing
This softback edition published in 2013 by Templar Publishing,
an imprint of The Templar Company Limited,
Deepdene Lodge, Deepdene Avenue, Dorking, Surrey, RH5 4AT, UK
www.templarco.co.uk

Copyright © 2012 by Yokococo

First softback edition

ISBN 978-1-84877-231-1

Edited by Hannah Wilson

Printed in Singapore

Yokococo

Hans and Matilda

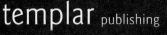

templar publishing

There was once a little cat

called Matilda.

And there was once a little cat
called Hans.

Th... so different...

Everyone said Matilda was such a **good** girl.

But people said, "Be quiet, Hans!"

Everyone said Matilda was such a **sweet** girl.

But people said,

"Stop it, Hans!"

Everyone said

Matilda was such a **thoughtful** girl.

But people said,

"Hans! How dare you!"

One night Hans went too far…

and climbed the gates of the zoo.

Hans borrowed a set of keys…

and set

all of the animals free!

"Oh dear!" said Matilda. "Naughty Hans!"

WANTED

$1000 REWARD

for information leading to the arrest of
a very naughty cat (answers to the name Hans).

Matilda decided that
something must be done.

"Excuse me," said Matilda.
"I know where Hans will be
at midnight tonight!"

"Thank you very much
for your information, Matilda,"
said the policeman.

On the stroke of midnight,

Hans was caught red-handed:

"Got you!"

shouted the policeman.

The policeman

took off

Hans's hat.

The policeman

took off

Hans's mask.

Finally, the policeman removed

Hans's whiskers.

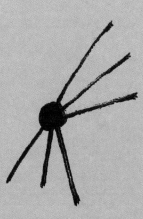

And, underneath them he found...

"Can I have my reward now please,

Mr. Policeman?"

said Matilda

in a **very** sweet voice.

And she promised to be

very, very good from then on

(unless, of course, she was wearing a hat,

and a mask, and some whiskers).